The Presents

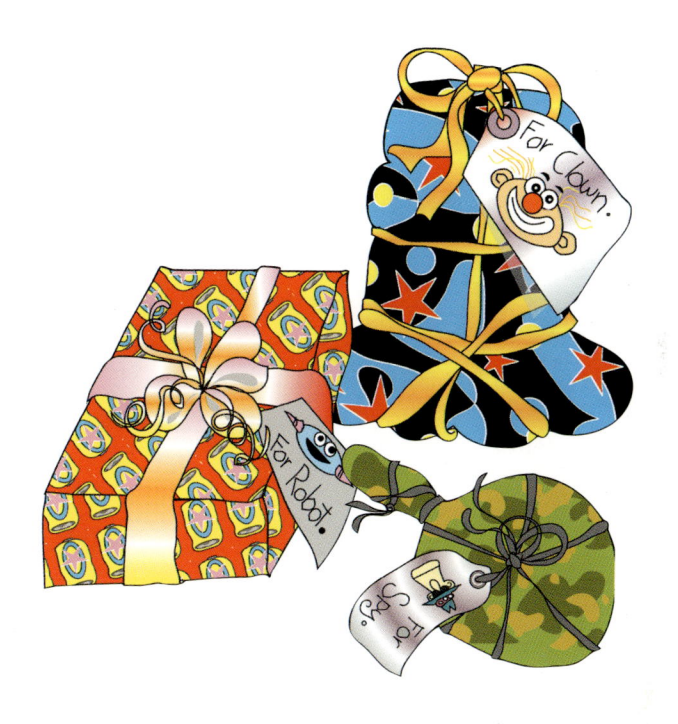

Illustrated by Jim Storey

Rigby

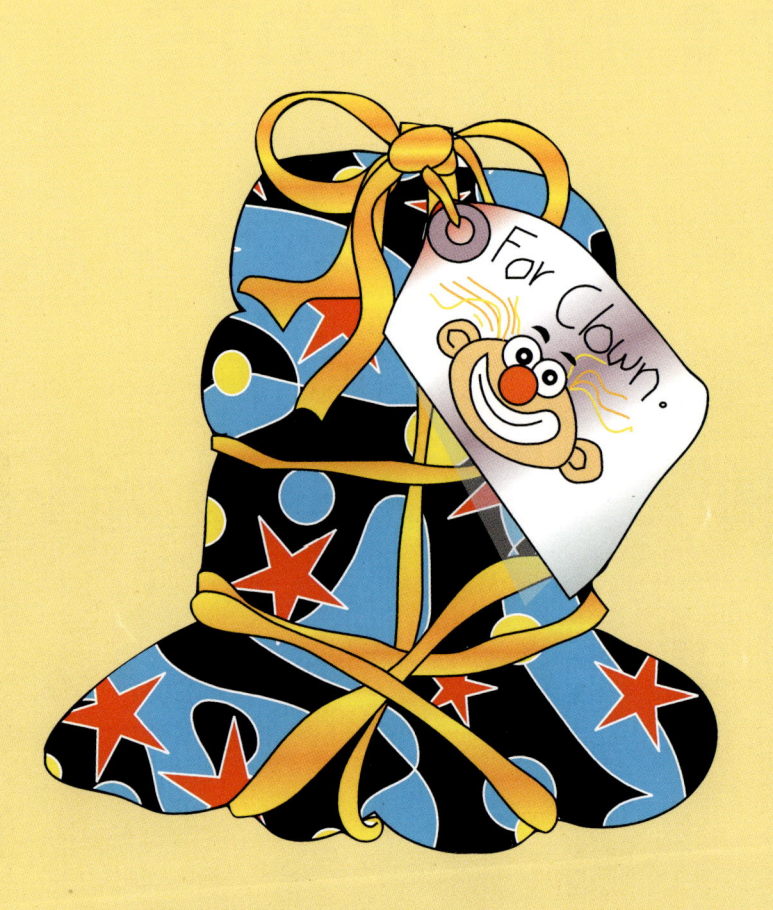

This is for
a clown.

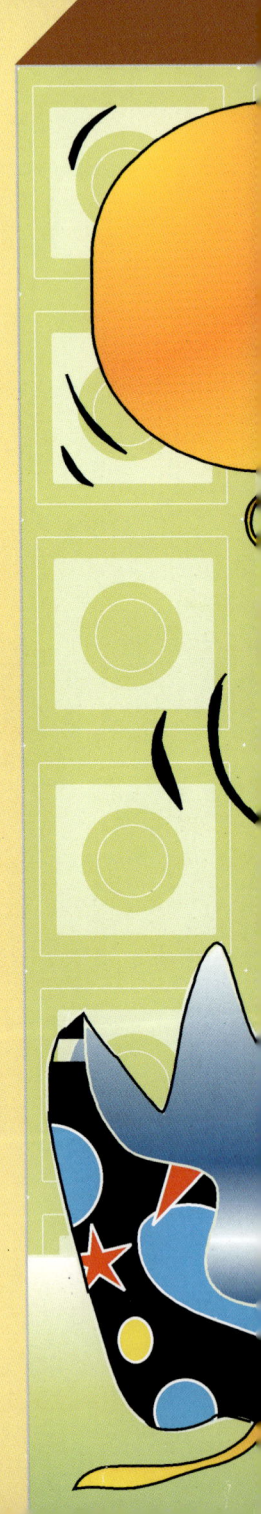

3

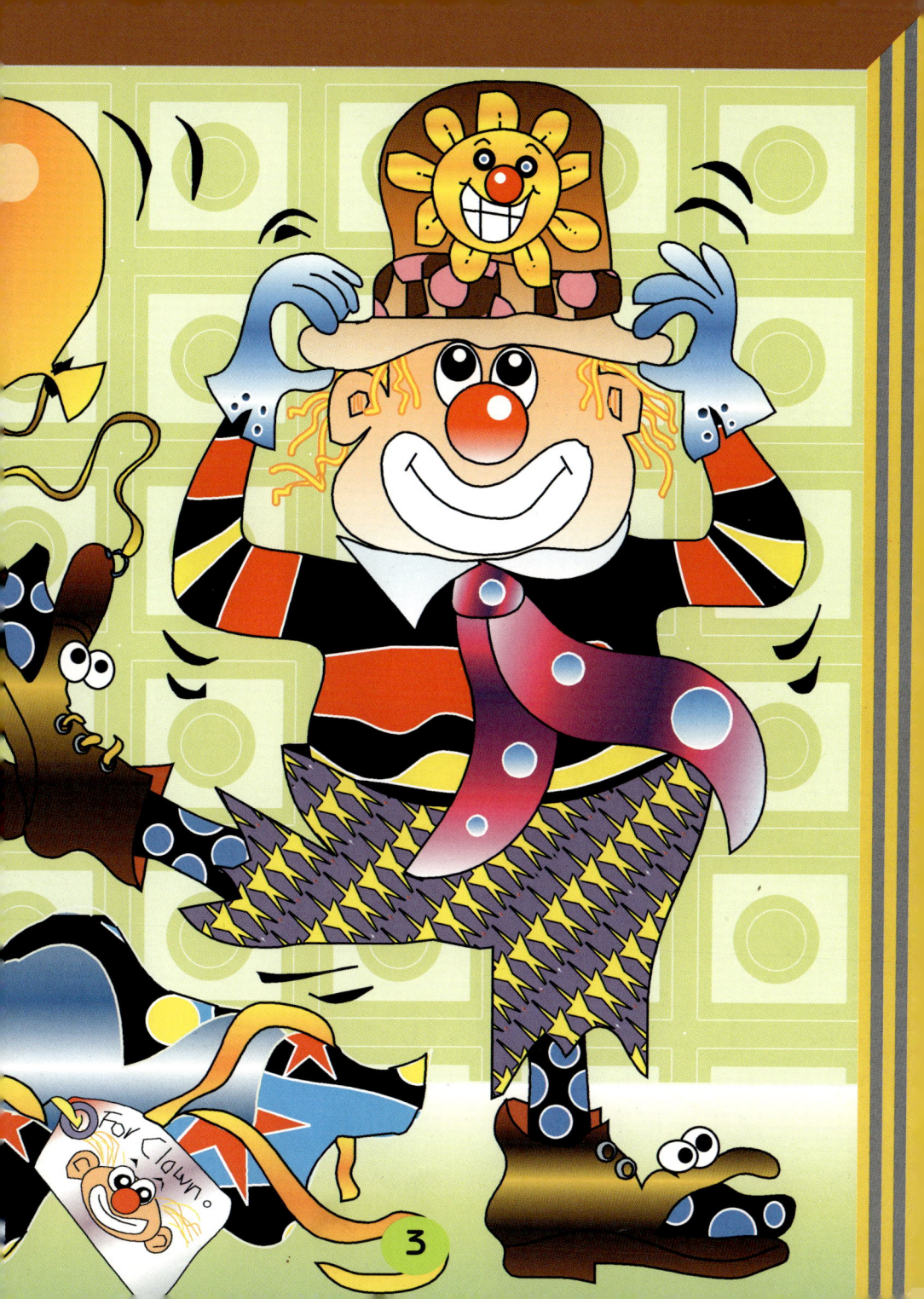

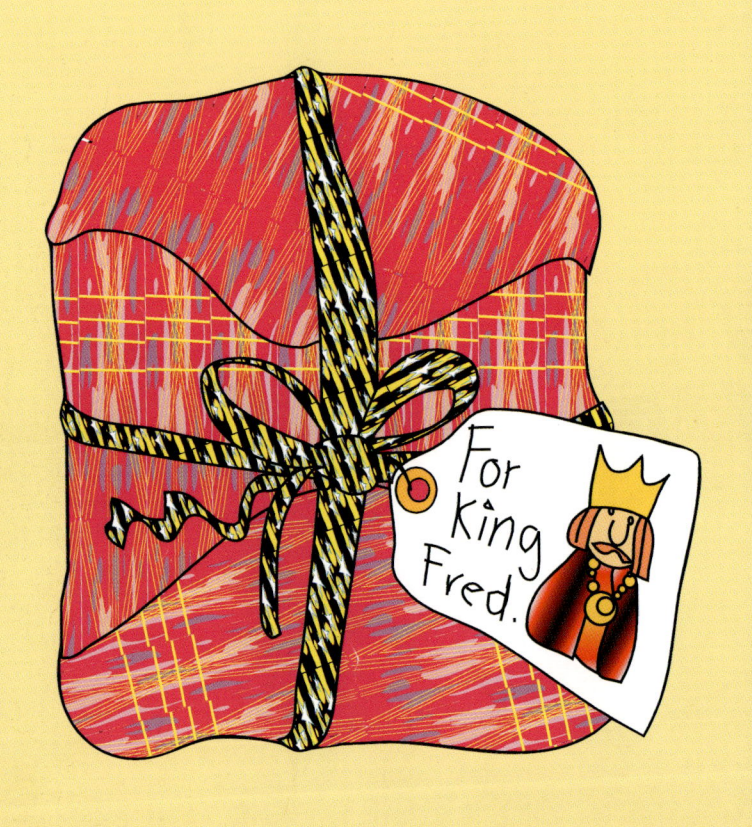

This is for
a king.

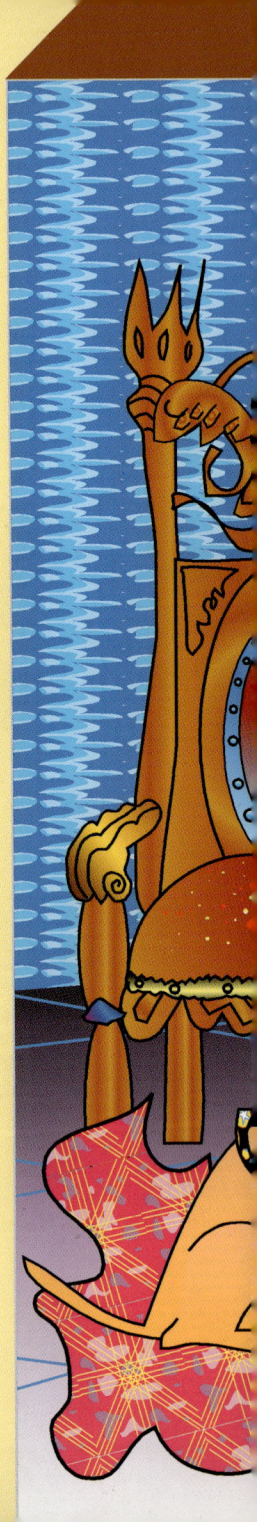

5

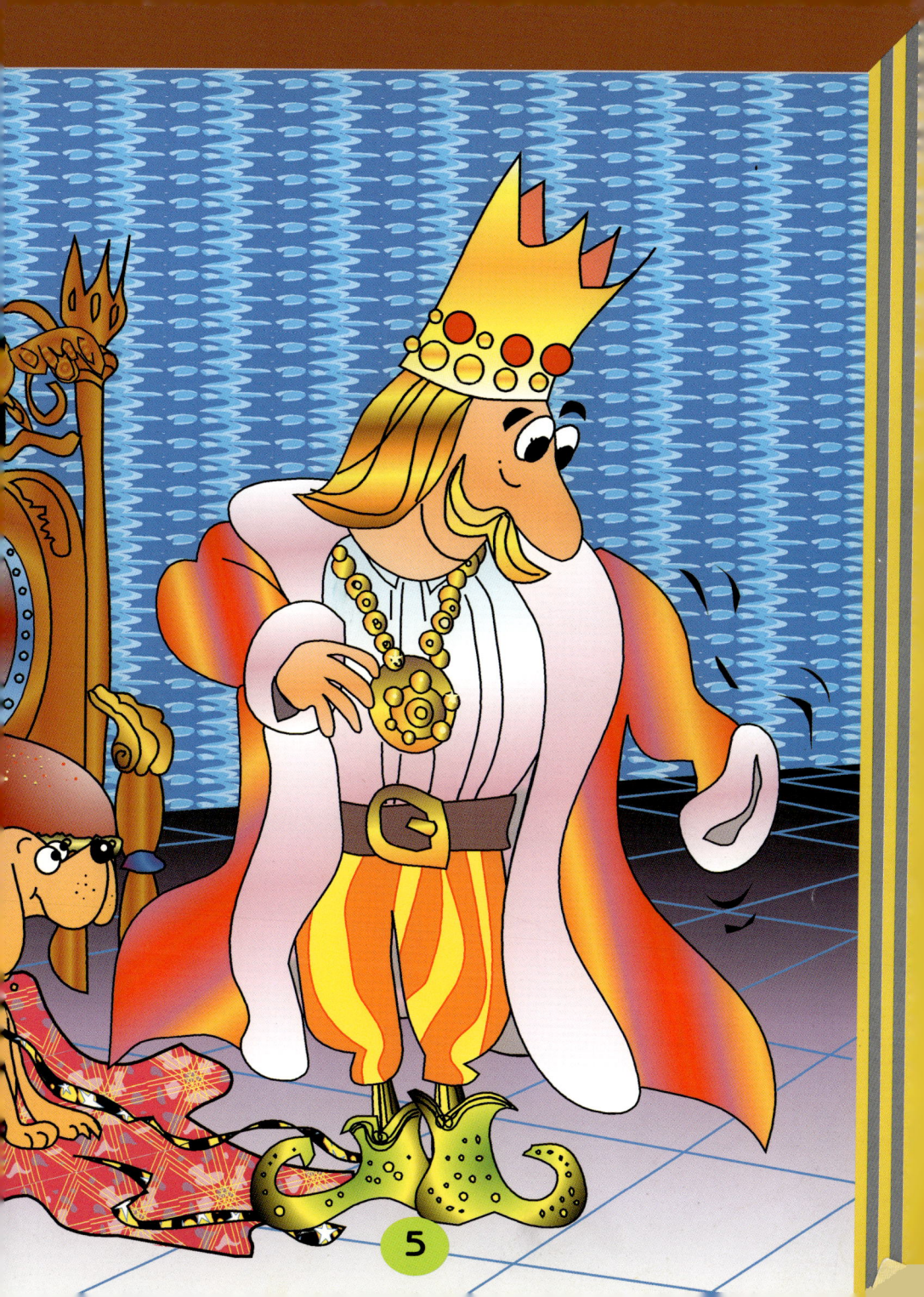

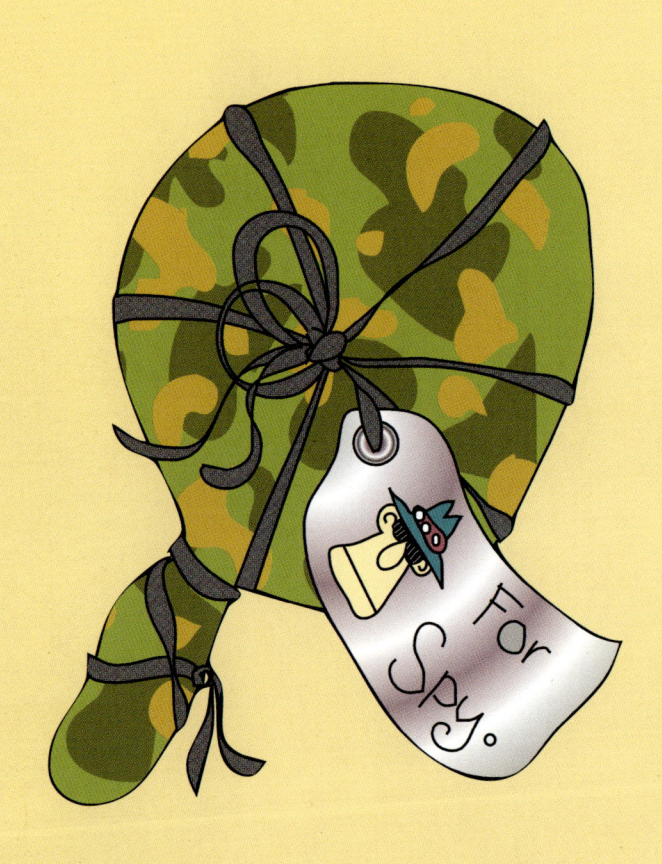

This is for
a spy.

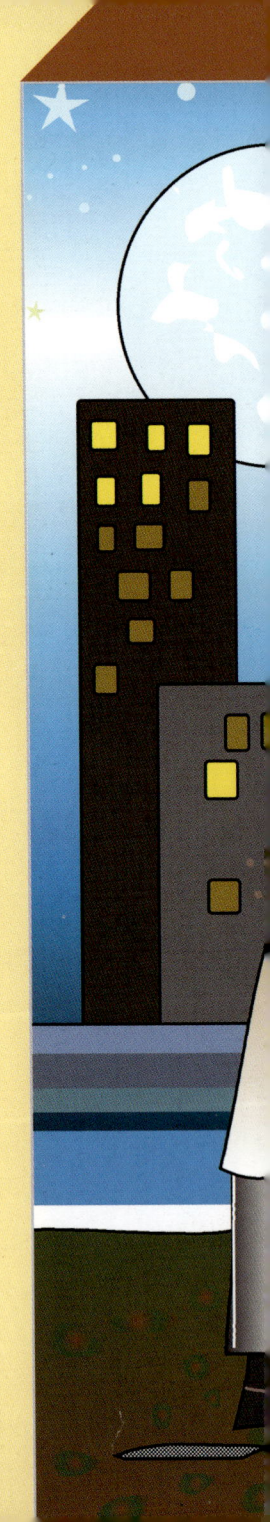

7

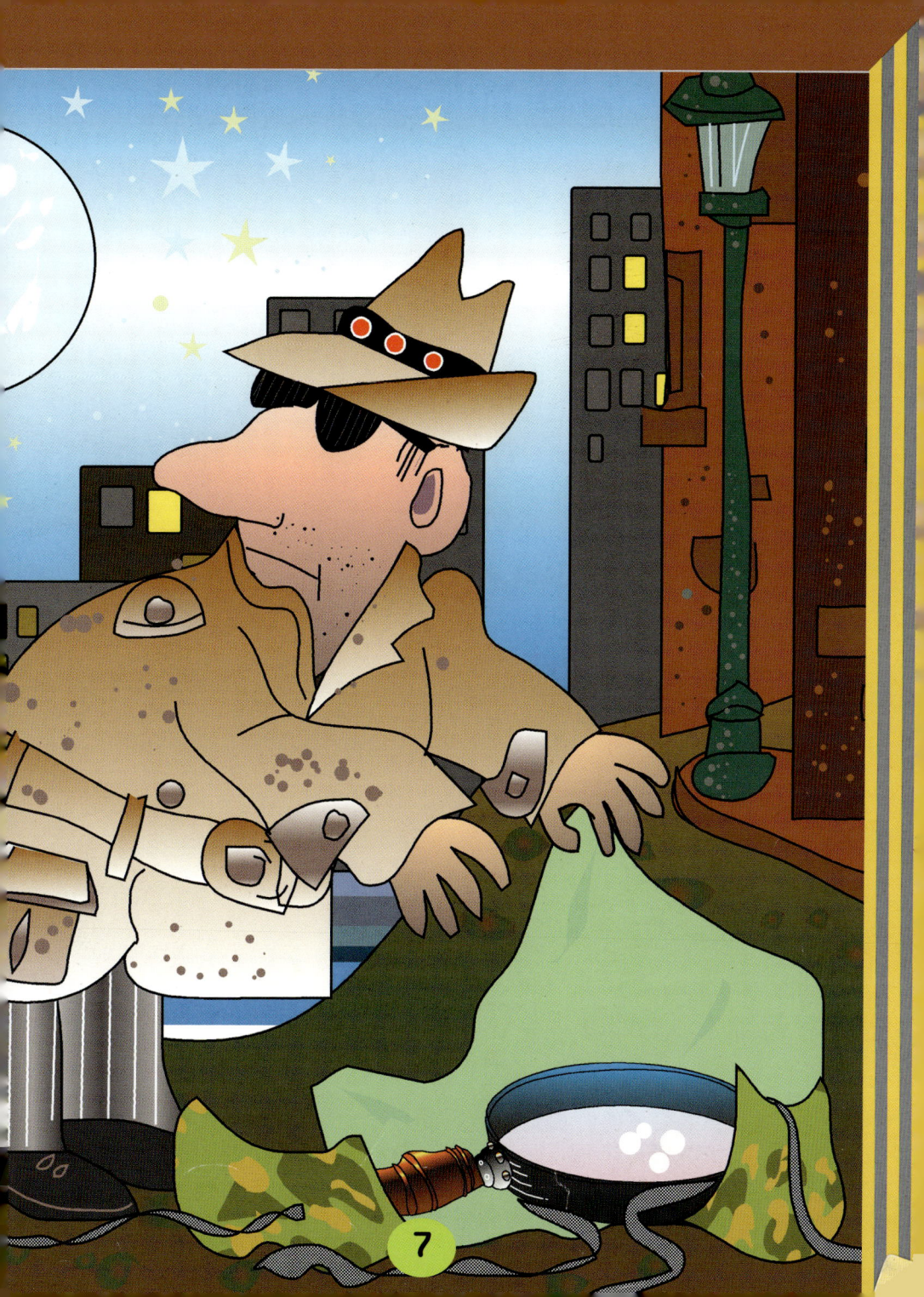

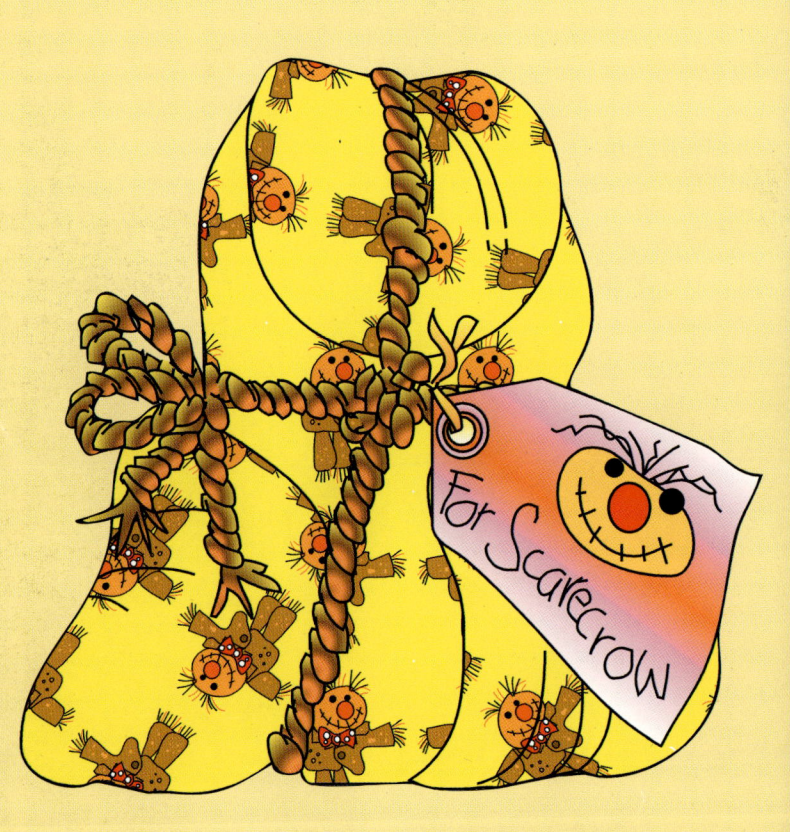

This is for
a scarecrow.

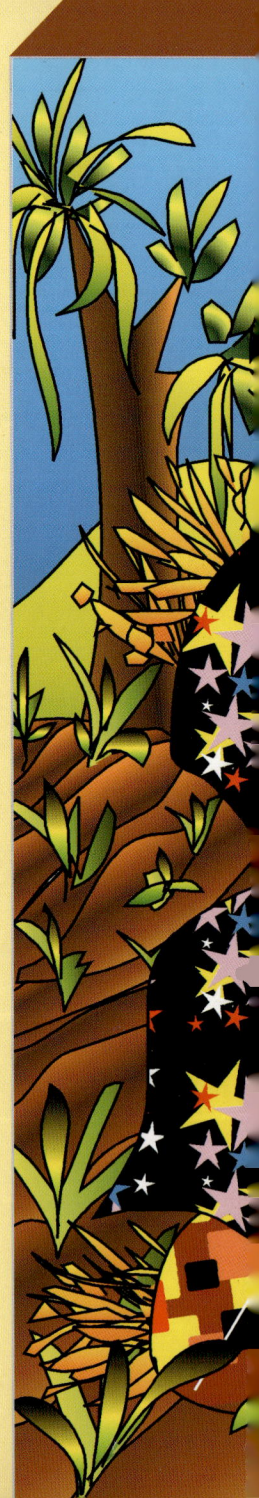

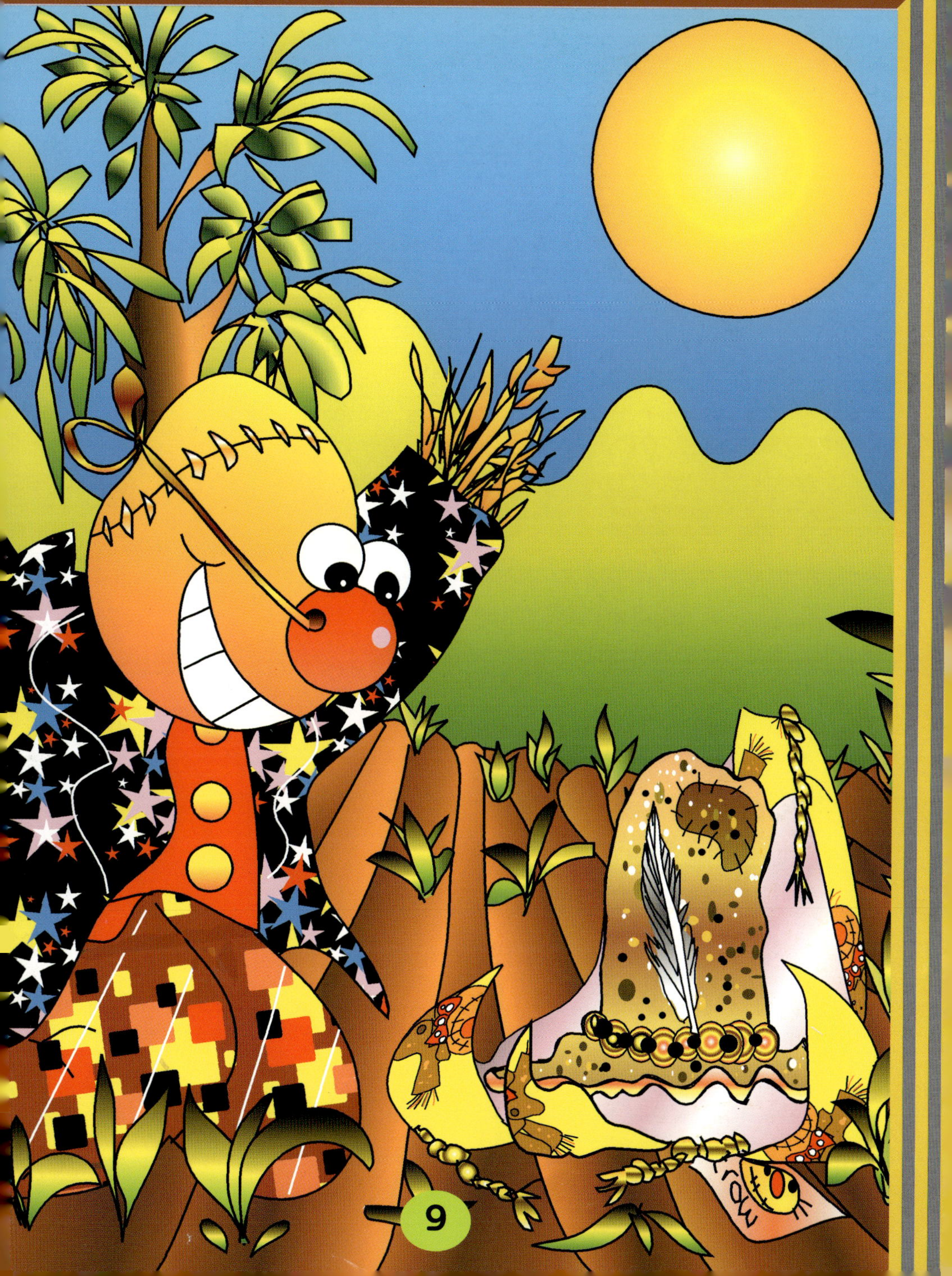

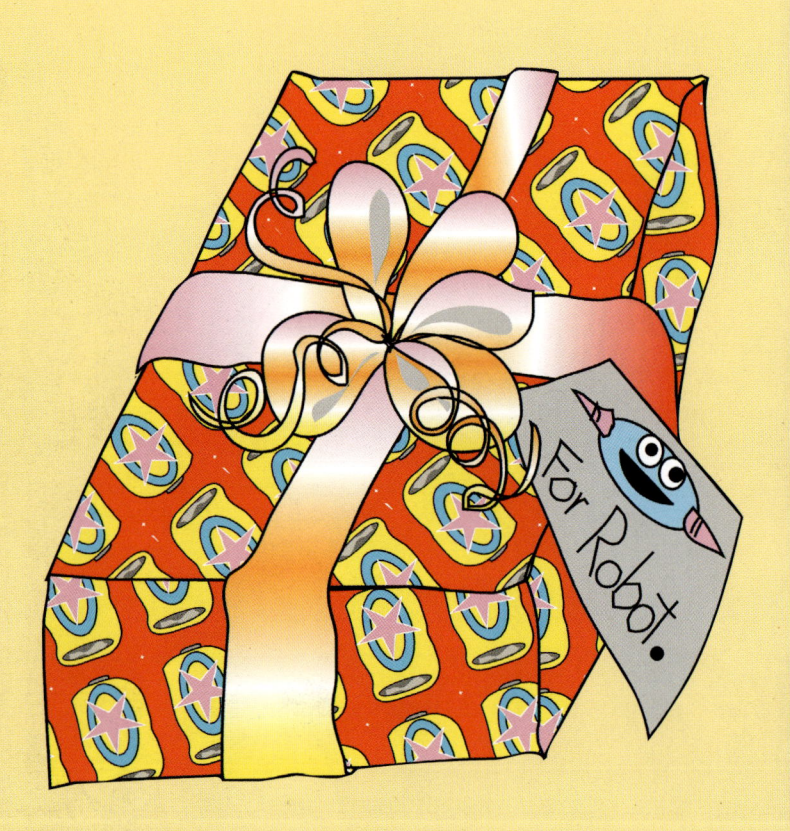

This is for a robot.

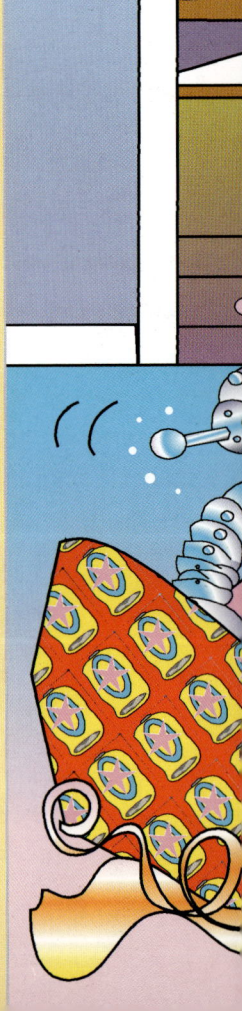

11

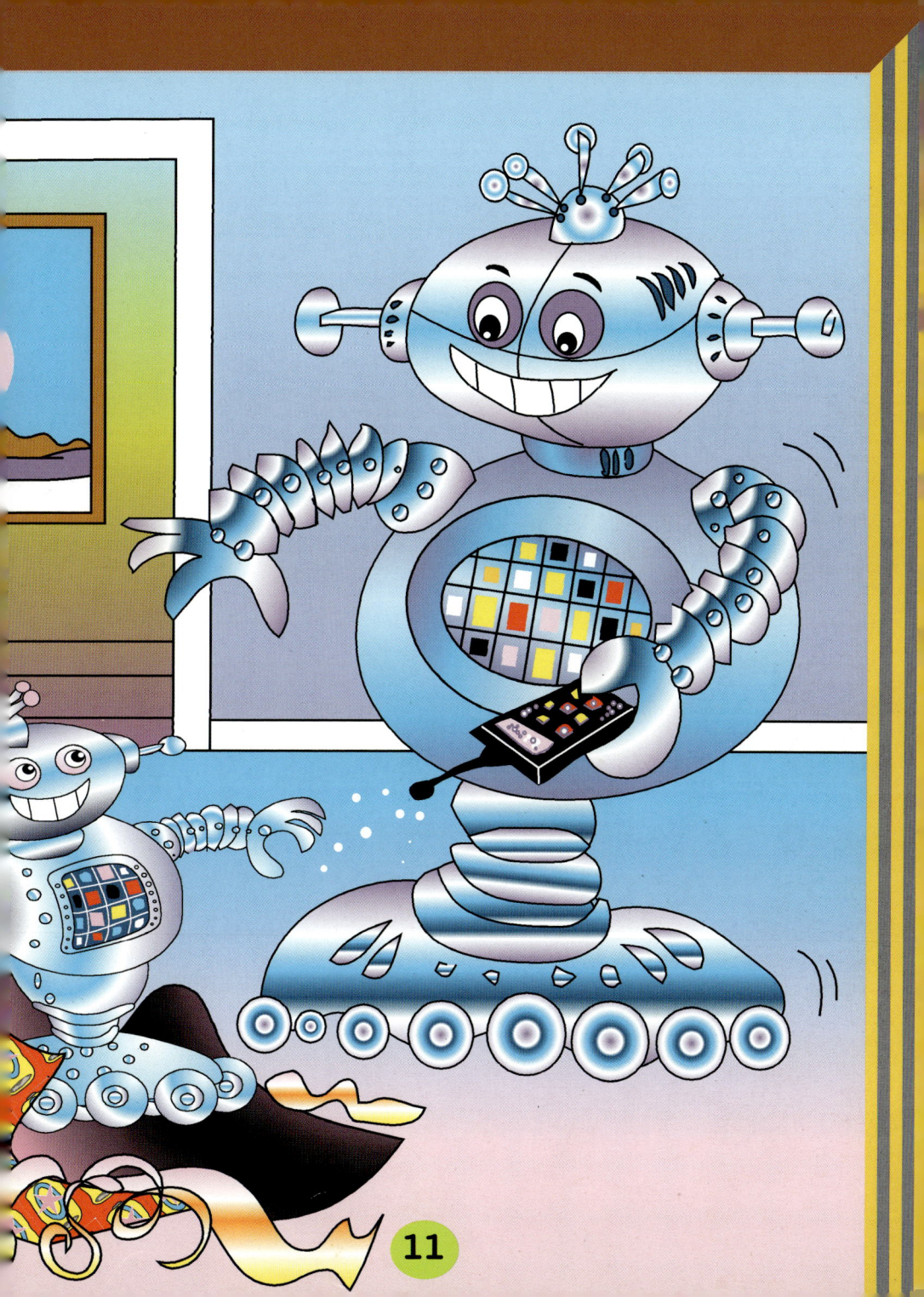

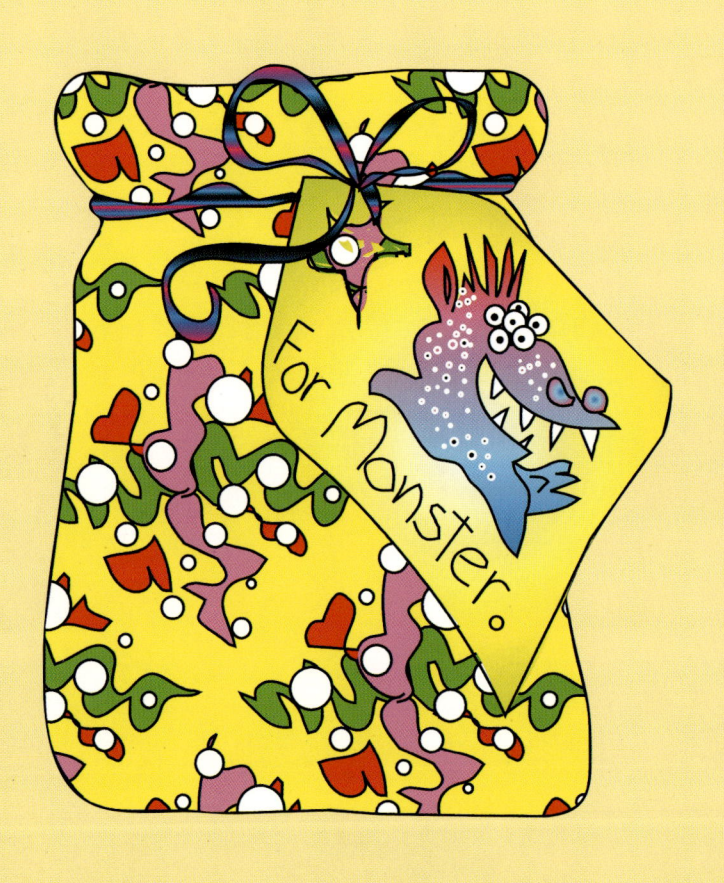

This is for
a monster.

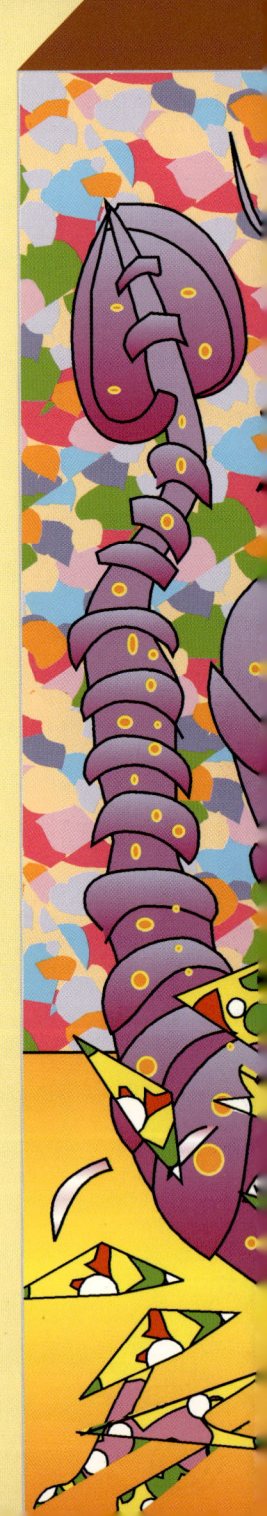

13

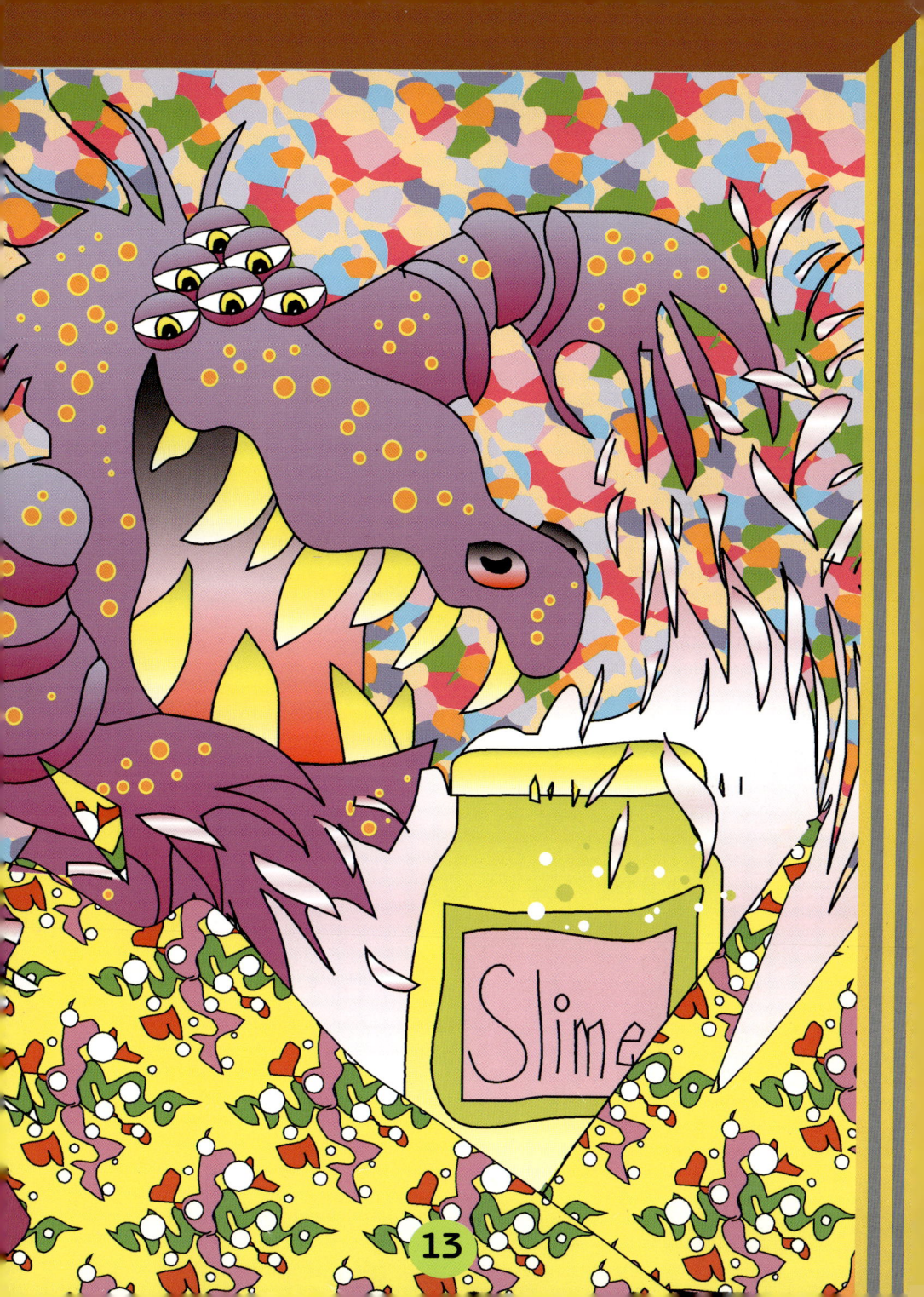

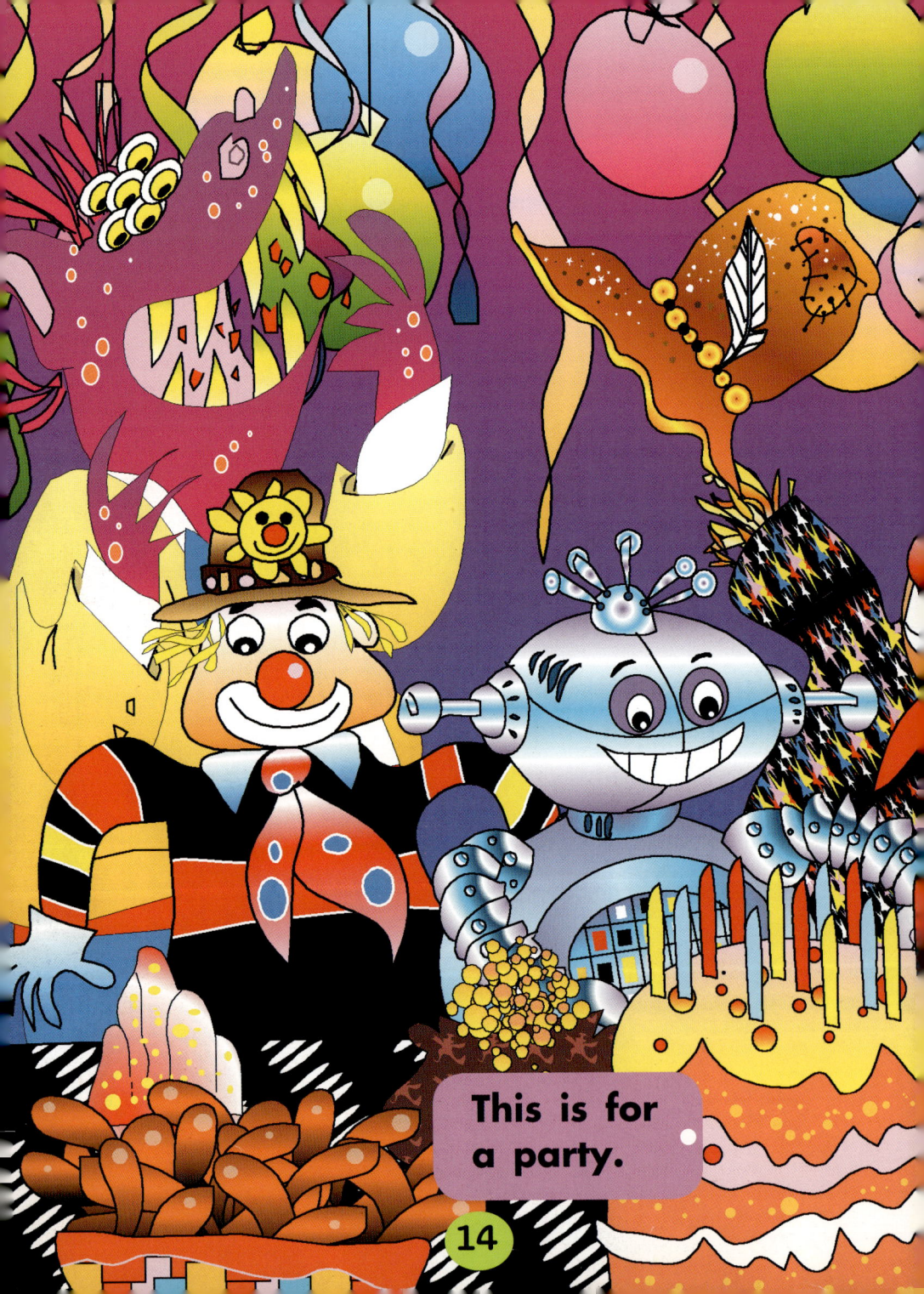

This is for a party.

15

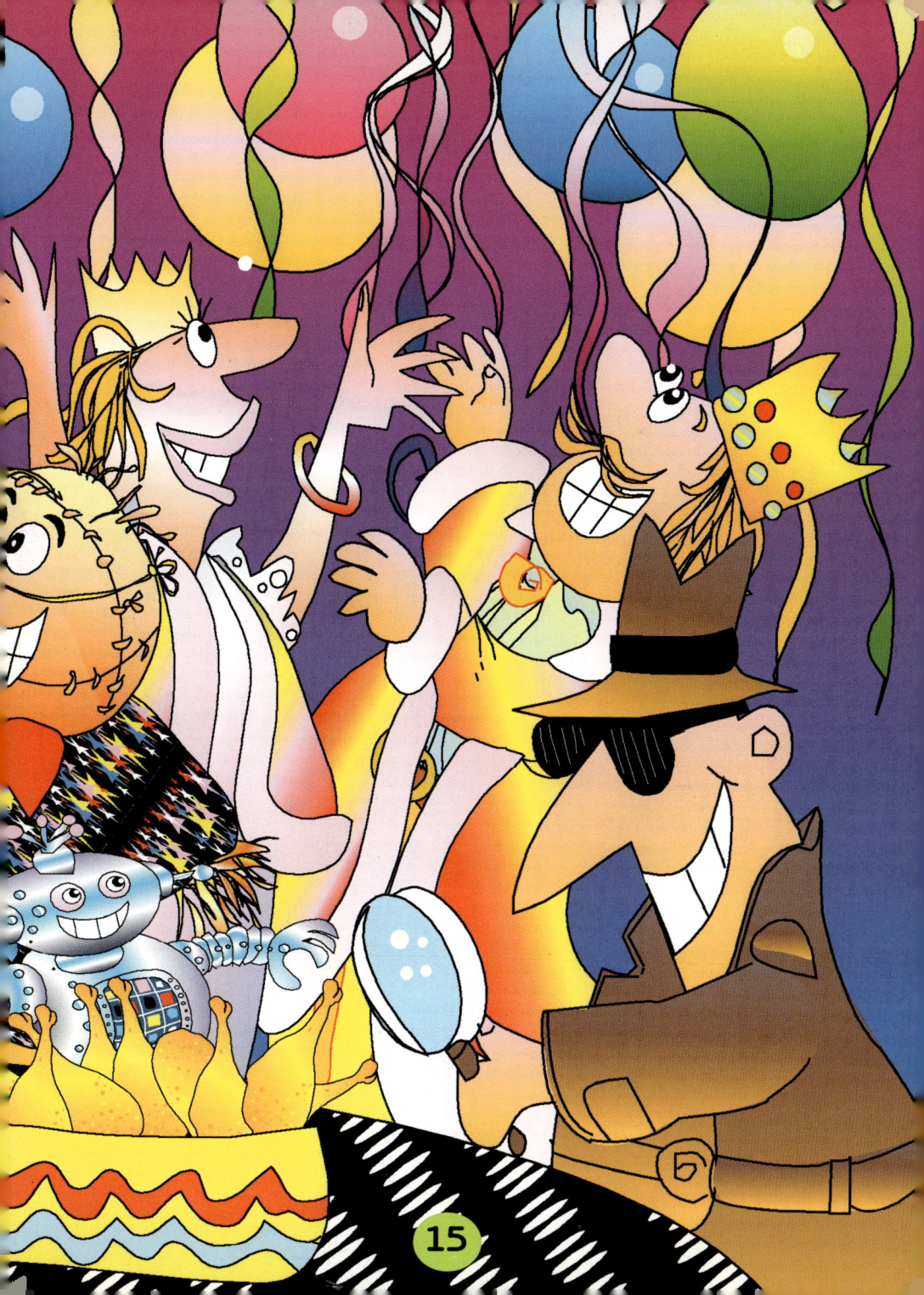

this

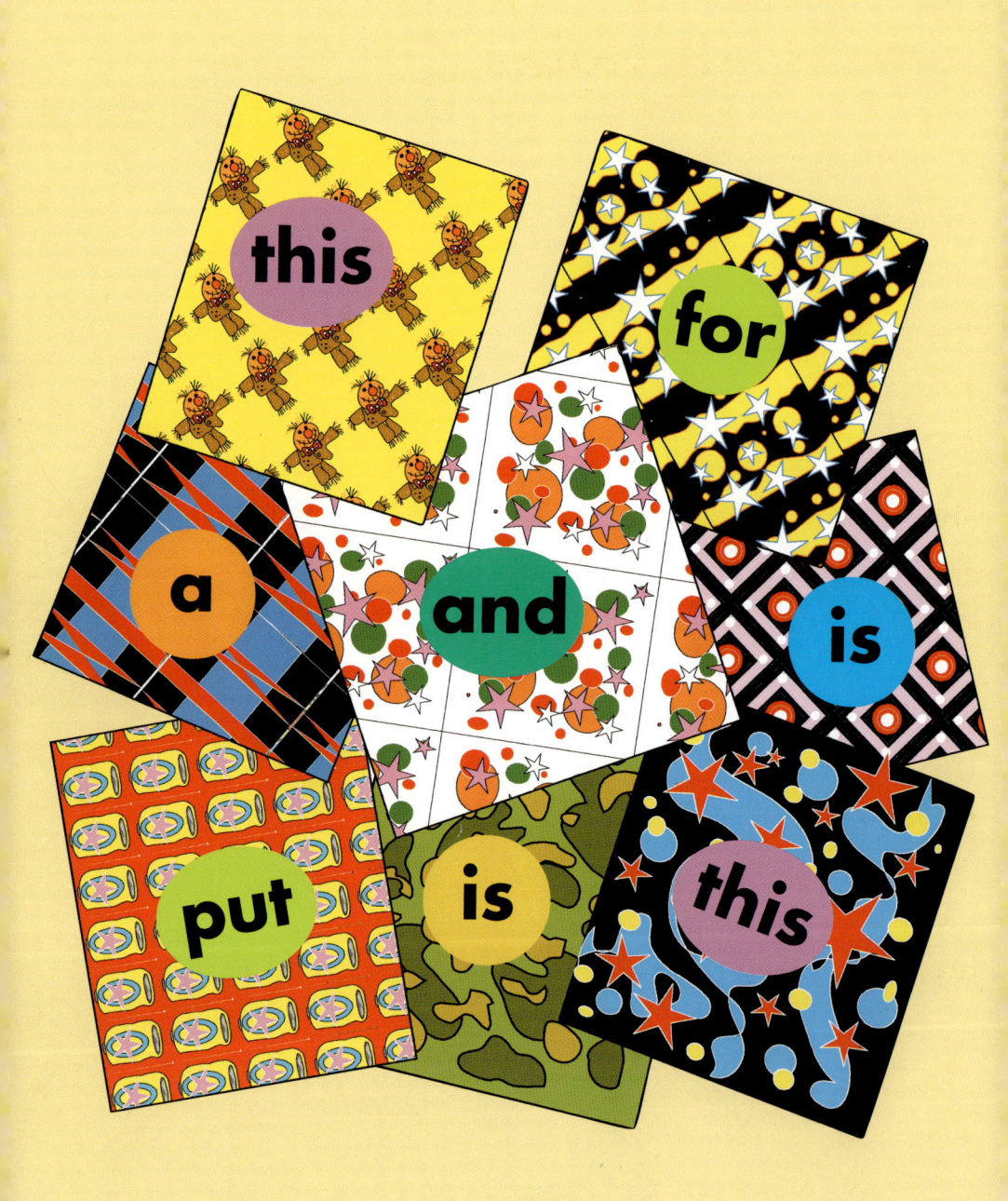

for

a

and

is

put

is

this